CAN YOU READ THIS BOOK?

Huw Lewis-Jones

CAN YOU
READ THIS
BOOK?

A BOOK OF NONSENSE TO
TWIST YOUR TONGUE TO

BRITISH LIBRARY

The English language is richly rewarding: SIMPLE & PLAYFUL, and sometimes terrifically confusing too. The love of this language has travelled the globe and brought people together. It's estimated over one billion of us on Earth now read and speak English, and millions are beginning to learn the language every day…

English is great fun to learn but at times it is also DELIBERATELY DIFFICULT. There is a long history of word play and challenge in using English words. Tongue-twisters, for example, are a great way to practise pronunciation, improve your confidence and develop your reading skills.

A TONGUE-TWISTER is a phrase or group of words that are sometimes tricky to say because of a sequence of similar sounds. They can be used as a kind of therapy as well as for play. They're not just for kids but are also used by film stars and TV presenters, and all kinds of people for warming up before perfectly delivering their lines.

This collection presents many English language favourites, some old and some newly made, to try twisting your tongue to. Each page becomes a mini challenge, dip in and out, or attempt to READ ALL THE WAY TO THE END in one sitting. The word gatherings get harder as the book goes on, but each gets easier, of course, once you have a go…

Read these words carefully and read them aloud. Try saying them as quickly as you can. Delight in the confusion and test yourself. You'll soon get the hang of it.

Can you read this book? I HOPE SO.

But,

CAN YOU CAN A
CAN AS A CANNER
CAN CAN A CAN?

Well, with a little practice, anyone can…

This is a book filled with WORDS. It might seem like a
serious book but it's not. It really is just about PLAYING
with words.

EASY WORDS

HARDER WORDS

FUNNY WORDS

CONFUSING WORDS

SHORTISH WORDS AND WOR

LOVELY-LONG-AND-LISTY

and

TRICKY-TRIP-UP-TANGLED

WORDS

DS LINED NEATLY IN A ROW

DS THAT

TUMBLE

AS THEY

GO

So, let's begin…
Do you know any
tongue-twisters?
I'm sure you do.

Let's start with something simple.
Repeat after me...

RED LORRY YELLOW LORRY

Easy-peasy.

Now, try saying it three times...

RED LORRY YELLOW LORRY
RED LORRY YELLOW LORRY
RED LORRY YELLOW LORRY

Well done.

Have another go, this time as QUICKLY as you can with no
mistakes...

...on your marks, get set, go!

REDLORRYYELLOWLORRYREDLORRY
REDLORRYYELLOWLORRYREDLORRY

Hey, not bad at all.

OWLORRYREDLORRYYELLOWLORRY
OWLORRYREDLORRYYELLOWLORRY

But it's quite tricky isn't it,
even for something so simple.
Let's try another…

BLUE BUBBLE BLACK BUBBLE

That was far too easy, I know.
You're already an expert.

Say it again, three times, nice and fast…

BLUE BUBBLE BLACK BUBBLE

BLUE BUBBLE BLACK BUBBLE

BLUE BUBBLE BLACK BUBBLE

Now, what if we play with the words a bit?

blue BUBBLE black BUBBLE

BLUE bubble BLACK bubble

BLUE bubble BLACK BUBBLE

Or, if we add some colour?

blue BUBBLE black BUBBLE

BLUE bubble BLACK bubble

BLUE bubble BLACK BUBBLE

Interesting.

What about this…

REDLORRYYELLOWLORRYREDLORRYYELLOWLORRY
REDLORRYYELLOWLORRYREDLORRYYELLOWLORRY
REDLORRYYELLOWLORRYREDLORRYYELLOWLORRY
REDLORRYYELLOWLORRYREDLORRYYELLOWLORRY
REDLORRYYELLOWLORRYREDLORRYYELLOWLORRY
REDLORRYYELLOWLORRYREDLORRYYELLOWLORRY
REDLORRYYELLOWLORRYREDLORRYYELLOWLORRY
REDLORRYYELLOWLORRYREDLORRYYELLOWLORRY
REDLORRYYELLOWLORRYREDLORRYYELLOWLORRY

Confusing I know.
But it's OK to make mistakes, you're only warming up.

Right, what next?

I'm sure you know this one…

SHE SELLS SEASHELLS

Shall we make it a little longer?

SHE SELLS SEASHELLS
ON THE SEASHORE
THE SHELLS THAT SHE SELLS
ARE SEASHELLS, I'M SURE

That's an old tongue-twister, had you heard it before?

Can you say **SEASHELLS** seven times?

Even that is pretty hard!

SEASHELLS SEASHELLS
SEASHELLS SEASHELLS
SEASHELLS SEASHELLS
SEASHELLS

What about this…

ELEVEN LEMON LOLLIES

Great.

Try saying it three times, as fast as you can.

ELEVEN LEMON LOLLIES
ELEVEN LEMON LOLLIES
ELEVEN LEMON LOLLIES

OK, what about...

ELEVEN LEMON LOLLIES
ELEVEN LEMON LOLLY LORRIES
ELEVEN LEMON LOLLY LORRIES
FULL OF LOVELY LEMON LOLLIES

Delicious.

But can you say LEMON LOLLY LORRIES eleven times?
I still can't.

Now, what about...

TWENTY-TWO TINY TURTLES
THIRTY-THREE THICK THISTLES
FORTY-FOUR FROZEN
   FRUITCAKES
FIFTY-FIVE FIERCE FISH
SIXTY-SIX SHORT STICKS
SEVENTY-SEVEN BENEVOLENT
   ELEPHANTS

Excellent.

By the way, BENEVOLENT means kind.
Our world certainly needs more kindness right now,
and more animals…

I love animals!
This book needs more ANIMALS too.

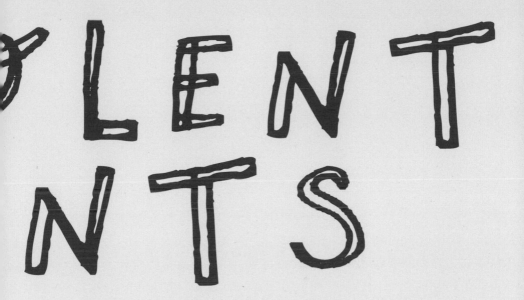

Let's imagine a menagerie.

What's a MENAGERIE? It's like a collection, a gathering of animals.

Have you heard the old rhyme TINKER, TAILOR, SOLDIER, SAILOR?

Instead, let's imagine an
imaginary menagerie...

PANDA
PUMA
BADGER
BEAVER

Try saying this without tripping up...

PANDAPUMABADGERBEAVER

PUMABEAVERPANDABADGER

BADGERPANDABEAVERPUMA

BEAVERBADGERPUMAPANDA

Quite tricky all stuck together like that.
Maybe they're cuddling.

Did you manage it?

OK, what about...

OTTEROYSTERLEMURLOBSTER
IGUANAIMPALACICADACHIHUAHUA

Do you know all of those animals?

A cicada is a little bug that sings really
loudly. You find lots of them in nice warm countries.
And a chihuahua is a kind of dog, but I always
spell it wrong!

Here are some more.
Can you say this all in one breath...

ALPACAANACONDABARRACUDABELUGA
CAPYBARACHINCHILLAGOPHERGORILLA
HYENAKOALAPANTHERPIRANHA
QUAGGAQUOKKATUNAVICUNA

All incredible creatures. Imagine the sounds!
A jungle-jumble of onomatopoeia!!
Wait - what's ONOMATOPOEIA?
It's the word we give to sounds that suggest the sounds
themselves.

Nice and noisy animal sounds, for example.
Like...

BUZZ CLUCK QUACK TWEET

Super simple, but can you say it quickly three times?

BUZZ CLUCK QUACK TWEET
BUZZ CLUCK QUACK TWEET
BUZZ CLUCK QUACK TWEET

Not so easy was it?

Animals do make some really awesome sounds...

BAA BARK CACKLE CAW
CHEEP CHIRP CUCKOO GOBBLE
HISS HONK HOOT HOWL
RIBBIT ROAR SCREECH SQUAWK
WARBLE WHINNY YIP YOWL

I bet you can think of many I'm missing!
Like...

BEARS GROWL BEES HUM AND BUZZ BEETLES
DRONE BIRDS SING BITTERNS BOOM CATS
MEOW AND MEW AND PURR CICADAS SING
AND CLICK COWS MOO DOGS BARK AND
WOOF AND ARF DOLPHINS CLICK AND
WHISTLE DONKEYS BRAY DOVES COO DUCKS
QUACK ELEPHANTS TRUMPET FROGS CROAK
GEESE CACKLE AND HISS AND HONK GUINEA
PIGS SQUEAK GULLS SQUAWK AND CRY
GRASSHOPPERS CHIRP HENS CLUCK HIPPOS
BRAY HORSES NEIGH HYENAS LAUGH, BUT
WHAT ABOUT A GIRAFFE?

KITTENS MEW LIONS ROAR LAMBS BLEAT
MONKEYS CHATTER OWLS HOOT AND
SCREECH AND TWIT-TWOO PIGEONS COO
PARROTS TALK PIGS GRUNT AND SQUEAL
RHINOS SNORT ROOKS CAW SANDPIPERS
PIPE AND WHISTLE SHEEP BLEAT AND BAA
SNAKES HISS SPARROWS CHIRP SWALLOWS
TITTER TORTOISES GRUNT SO I'M TOLD
TURKEYS GOBBLE TIGERS ROAR AND GROWL,
AND WOLVES HOWL!

we all know that bees buzz and cows go moo, but what about a zebra?

And I thought wolves *WHISTLE*, don't they?

Anyhow. While we're on the subject of animals, and I know you're pretty good at reading words and speaking sounds now, can you help me with something...

...how do we *SPELL* the sound an *OWL* makes?

TWIT-TWOO?

Does that sound right to you?
What about...

TO-WHIT-TO-WHOOO?

TOO-WHIT-TOO-WHOOO?

WHEEET-WHOOOOOOOOO?

PHWWWWWHHHT-PHWOOOOOH?

What about the sound a regular whistle makes? I'm thinking of a toy whistle. How do you even write a whistle, anyway?

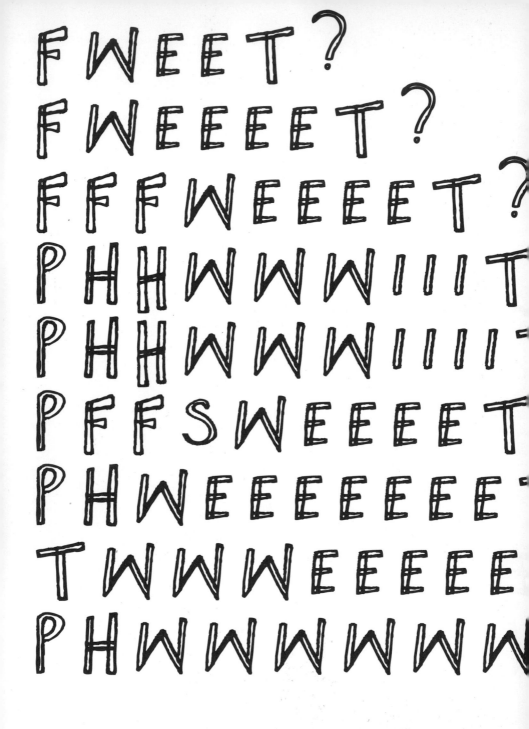

Now what about a referee's whistle?
Or, the whistle when a kettle boils for tea?
Or, if you're wearing false teeth,
I think it's more like PHWW—WIIIIIIITTTHH!

Can you read these whistling sounds…

PEEEEEP!
SEEEEEP!
SHFEEEEEETH!
PHWEEEEEEP!
SWEEEEEETH!
SHWEEEEEEEP!
SHFEEEEEEESSSTH!
WAWAWAAAAHOOHWA!
SHWEEEEEEEE-SHWEEEEEEEE!
WEETWOOHWEETTWEETWOOHWO
FFFWWWWWWHHHHHHHHEEEEEEEE
UUUUUUUUUUEEEEEEEEEEEEEHHHH
WHPHHHAAAEEEUUUEEEEEEOOOOO
OOOOOOOOOOOOOOOOOOOOOOOO
OOOOOOOOOOOOOOOOOOOEEEEEOOOEE

Goodness, this is getting
complicated.

WOOOH!

EEEEEEEEEUEEEEEEEEEEEEEEAAAAAAAAA

HHHHHHHH!

OOOOOOOOOOOOOOOOOOOOOOOOOO

EEEEEEEEEEEEEEEOOOOOOOOOOOO

WWWWWPHHH!

I know this is a bit ridiculous, but let's keep going.
Let's try some simpler sounds.
In fact, some of my favourite words are SIMPLE short
sound words.

Like…

BUBBLE

and...

SIZZLE

Can we make up a tongue-twisting kind of rhyme?

BUBBLE BUBBLE DOUBLE BUBBLE
DOUBLE DOUBLE BUBBLE TROUBLE
SIZZLE SIZZLE FIZZLE SIZZLE
FIZZLE FIZZLE SIZZLE SWIZZLE

Or what about...

SIZZLE SIZZLE SAUSAGE SIZZLE

BUSY SIZZLING IN THE DRIZZLE

DRIZZLY DRIZZLE

MIST AND MIZZLE

SAUSAGE SIZZLE FIZZLE SWIZZLE

BUBBLE BUBBLE TOILET TROUBLE

CALL THE PLUMBER

AT THE DOUBLE

MUDDLE MEDDLE FIDDLE FUDDLE

TOILET TROUBLE PIDDLE PUDDLE

Doesn't make much sense.
Sorry, I tried.

Anyway, what's your FAVOURITE word?
Can you make up a nice and tricky rhyme about it?

Some of my other favourite words just feel nice in the
mouth. Try saying these loud and proud...

PEBBLE PUDDLE
BABBLE BRAMBLE
FIDDLE FUDDLE
MIDDLE MUDDLE
DOODLE NOODLE
STRUDEL POODLE
MUMBLE CRUMBLE
BOBBLE BUMBLE

That sounded great!
YOU sounded great!

People make all sorts of interesting sounds.
Can you think of any?

What about saying all of these in one go...

CHOO
HEM
HOY AHA
LAB BRRRR BURP
CHATTER CHOMP CHORTLE CHUCKLE
GARGLE GIGGLE GROAN GRUNT GRUMBLE
HICCUP HUM HUSH MOAN MURMUR MUTTER
SCREAM SHOUT SIGH SLOBBER SLURP
SNIFF SNORT SQUEAL WAFFLE
WOW WOAH WHISPER
YAY YIKES
YAWN
ZZZZ

YOU sounded great. Again!

And it's not just people. THINGS make all sorts of
wonderful sounds too.

I'm sure you can think of loads.

Here are some of my favourites. Take a deep
breath and try to say them all in one go…

BAM BANG BASH BEEP BOING BUMP CLANG

CLUNK CRACK CRACKLE CRASH CREAK C

FLUTTER GLUG GURGLE PLINK PLONK P

RING RUFF RUMBLE RUSTLE SLAP SLIP S

SPLAT SPLATTER SPLUTTER SPLISH SP

THUD THUMP THWACK TINKLE TRICKLE

WHIP WHIR WHIZ WHOOP WHOOSH ZAP

Wow.
Did you manage it?

ANK CLASH CLATTER CLICK CLINK
K CRUNCH DRIP FIZZ FLICK FLIP
PLUCK PLUNK POP POW PUFF RATTLE
HER SLOP SLOSH SMASH SNIP SPLASH
SQUISH SQUELCH SWISH SWOOSH
NG VROOM WALLOP WHACK WHAM
ZIP ZOOOOOOOOM!

That was just great. To which I would only add...

BING-BONG DING-DONG
TICK-TOCK CLIP-CLOP
CLICKETY-CLACK
JINGLE-JANGLE
PITTER-PATTER PING-PONG
KAPOW KERPLUNK KABOOM!

OK!

Are you tired yet?

What time is it?

TICK-TOCK TALL CLOCK

Three times please…

TICK-TOCK TALL CLOCK

TICK-TOCK TALL CLOCK

TICK-TOCK TALL CLOCK

Ok, what about some other kinds of clock…can you say this in less than ten seconds…?

TICK-TOCK TALL CLOCK

TICK-TOCK SMALL CLOCK

TICK-TOCK TINY CLOCK

TICK-TOCK SHINY CLOCK

Nice! OK, add in a few more…

TICK-TOCK NEW CLOCK

TICK-TOCK BLUE CLOCK

TICK-TOCK OLD CLOCK

TICK-TOCK GOLD CLOCK

TALL SMALL TINY SHINY
  NEW BLUE OLD GOLD
NEW OLD BLUE GOLD
  SHINY SMALL TINY TALL

WOODEN CLOCK CUCKOO CLOCK
HANGING ON THE WALL
TICKING CLOCK TOCKING CLOCK
CAN YOU SAY THEM ALL?

And, time's up!

Phew. Let's take a break and sit down for a bit…

A SKUNK SAT ON A STUMP
AND THUNK THE STUMP STUNK
BUT THE STUMP THUNK THE
SKUNK STUNK

As we're now in the WOODS, why not try...

THE BIG BLACK BEAR SITTING
BY THE BIG BLACK BUG

ROUND AND ROUND THE RUGGED
ROCKS THE RAGGED RASCAL RAN

PROFESSIONAL PUMPKIN PICKERS
ARE PRONE TO PICK THE
PLUMPEST PUMPKINS
...POSSIBLY?

Actually, I don't know the answer to that!

But it does bring us to some CLASSIC
tongue-twisting questions...

IF A DOG CHEWS SHOES, WHOSE SHOES DOES HE CHOOSE?

CAN YOU CAN A CAN AS A CANNER CAN CAN A CAN?

HOW MUCH WOOD WOULD A WOODCHUCK CHUCK IF A WOODCHUCK COULD CHUCK WOOD?

A TUTOR WHO TOOTED A FLUTE TRIED TO TUTOR TWO TOOTERS TO TOOT.
SAID THE TWO TO THEIR TUTOR, "IS IT HARDER TO TOOT OR TO TUTOR TWO TOOTERS TO TOOT?"

Or what about this really OLD tongue-twister…

PETER PIPER PICKED A PECK
  OF PICKLED PEPPERS.
A PECK OF PICKLED PEPPERS
  PETER PIPER PICKED.
IF PETER PIPER PICKED A PECK
  OF PICKLED PEPPERS,
WHERE'S THE PECK OF PICKLED
  PEPPERS PETER PIPER PICKED?

Know it?

People have been trying to say it for well over two
hundred years! It is, perhaps, the most FAMOUS tongue-
twister of all. It's really good that you've said it now.

Here's another old one, this time from America, but I
often struggle to get it right...

BETTY BOTTER BOUGHT SOME BUTTER,
BUT THE BUTTER, IT WAS BITTER.
IF SHE PUT IT IN HER BATTER,
IT WOULD MAKE HER BATTER BITTER,
BUT A BIT OF BETTER BUTTER,
THAT WOULD MAKE HER BATTER BETTER.
SO, SHE BOUGHT A BIT OF BUTTER,
BETTER THAN HER BITTER BUTTER,
AND SHE PUT IT IN HER BATTER,
AND HER BATTER WAS NOT BITTER.
SO, T'WAS BETTER BETTY BOTTER
BOUGHT A BIT OF BETTER BUTTER.

Right, I'm exhausted.

Let's change direction for a bit and try a simple word
puzzle.

Can you read this?

BOW BOW BOW BOW

> That sounded nice, but sorry it was
> not quite right. Have another go.

Your way was good, but you didn't read it how I wrote it.
Can you do it a different way?

BOW BOW BOW BOW

> Sorry, that was good but wrong again.

Does this clue help?

BOAT RIBBON BOAT RIBBON

Confused? Try again...

BOW BOW BOW BOW

Got it this time? What about this clue...

BOAT RIBBON APPLAUSE ARROW

BOW BOW BOW BOW

That's BOW (as in the front of a boat) BOW (as in tying a ribbon) BOW (which you might do when you earn some applause) and BOW (which goes with an arrow). Get it?

It sounds like B—OWWW B—OWE B—OWWW B—OWE.

Now, knowing what you know, can you say more with these clues...

BOAT RIBBON APPLAUSE ARROW
BOAT APPLAUSE RIBBON ARROW
APPLAUSE BOAT APPLAUSE BOAT
ARROW RIBBON ARROW RIBBON

Does it help if I write it out for you?

BOW BOW BOW BOW
BOW BOW BOW BOW
BOW BOW BOW BOW
BOW BOW BOW BOW

No, didn't think it would!

Try saying your BOWS and BOWS again...

BOAT RIBBON APPLAUSE ARROW
BOAT APPLAUSE RIBBON ARROW
APPLAUSE BOAT APPLAUSE BOAT
ARROW RIBBON ARROW RIBBON

Whoohoo!
That was quite hard wasn't it? Take a BOW!

I get it wrong almost every time.
Did you find it easy?

OK, smarty-pants.
Try this, as FAST as you possibly can...

BIG ISSUES
BIGGER SHOES
SMALL ISSUES
SMALLER SHOES
TEN ISSUES
TENNIS SHOES

Good.

OK. Let's recap. You remember this…

RED LORRY YELLOW LORRY

How many times can you say it now?
Are you getting tired, or is it getting easier
…and QUICKER?

Now, let's do a whole bunch of tongue-twisters in rapid
fire.

Like a tongue-twisting assault course. To start with these
are best said QUICKLY three times. But feel free to
test your skills! See how many times you can say them
before falling over…

…on your marks, get set, go!

FIT DOG FAT DOG
FIT DOG FAT DOG
FIT DOG FAT DOG
THIN CAT THICK CAT
THIN CAT THICK CAT
THIN CAT THICK CAT
ROLLING RED WAGONS
ROLLING RED WAGONS
ROLLING RED WAGONS
SNAP CRACKLE POP
SNAP CRACKLE POP
SNAP CRACKLE POP
TOP COP
TOP COP
TOP COP
SLIP SLAP SLOP
SLIP SLAP SLOP
SLIP SLAP SLOP
BLACK BACKED BAT
BLACK BACKED BAT
BLACK BACKED BAT

GARGLING GARGOYLES

GARGLING GARGOYLES

GARGLING GARGOYLES

WORLD WIDE WEB

WORLD WIDE WEB

WORLD WIDE WEB

KNAPSACK STRAPS

KNAPSACK STRAPS

KNAPSACK STRAPS

FORK HANDLES FOUR CANDLES

FORK HANDLES FOUR CANDLES

FORK HANDLES FOUR CANDLES

RED LEATHER YELLOW LEATHER

RED LEATHER YELLOW LEATHER

RED LEATHER YELLOW LEATHER

TOY BOAT

TOY BOAT

TOY BOAT

You made it!!!

Let's just try that last one again.

TOY BOAT

It looks easy but it's super hard if you say it lots.
So, how many times can you say TOY BOAT?

Here it is just three times.

TOY BOAT
TOY BOAT
TOY BOAT

You might like to know, the world record for saying
TOY BOAT out loud and without mistakes is
twenty-two times!

Can you do it…

TOY BOAT TOY BOAT TOY BOAT
TOY BOAT TOY BOAT TOY BOAT
TOY BOAT TOY BOAT TOY BOAT
TOY BOAT TOY BOAT TOY BOAT
TOY BOAT TOY BOAT TOY BOAT
TOY BOAT TOY BOAT TOY BOAT
TOY BOAT TOY BOAT TOY BOAT

(Actually, I made that up. Sorry. I have no idea what the world record is.) Anyway, you're a champion in my eyes now, so what about these LINES next.

Race through them without speaking any mistakes…

SHE SEES CHEESE
SEVEN SWANS SWAM IN THE SEA
A NOISY NOISE ANNOYS AN OYSTER
THE CHEAP SHOP SOLD SHEEP CHOPS
NIGHT NURSE NELLY IS NURSING NICE
MY MISS MISSY MISSES MISSISSIPPI
MOSES SUPPOSES HIS TOESES ARE RO
SURELY WE SHALL SEE THE SUNSHINE
THIS FRIENDLY PHILIP FLIPS FINE FLAP
THAT FAT FRIAR FRED IS FRYING FRE
GREEN COWS GATHER TO GRAZE ON
A SHIP-SHIPPING SHIP SHIPPING SHIPP
CLEOPATRA'S MATTRESS HAS PINK AN
WE WENT TO WALES TO WATCH WHA
HORTENSE'S TORTOISE TAUGHT US T

N

KS

LOUNDER

N GRASS

SHIPS

RPLE PATCHES

ND WALRUS WINKING

MPORTANCE OF SHORTNESS

We're almost done.
I know you think this is all a bit ridiculous…
Maybe it's time for a HOLIDAY!

Okey-dokey. What shall we pack?

A BOX OF BISCUITS

A BATCH OF MIXED BISCUITS

A BIG BOTTLE

A BLUE BOTTLE

A BROWN BOTTLE

A BABY BOTTLE

A SWISS WRISTWATCH

AN IRISH WRISTWATCH

A FRENCH FLIPFLOP

A TURQUOISE TOOTHBRUSH

SEVEN SLIPPERY SNAILS

SIX SILK SKIRTS

FIVE FRANTIC FROGS

AND A PROPER COPPER COFFEE POT

Not all that useful, I know.
But, we don't want to forget anything.

Let's check again...

BOX OF BISCUITS MIXED BISCUITS
BIG BOTTLE BLUE BOTTLE BROWN
BOTTLE BABY BOTTLE SWISS
WRISTWATCH IRISH WRISTWATCH
FRENCH FLIPFLOP TURQUOISE
TOOTHBRUSH SLIPPERY SNAILS
SILK SKIRTS FRANTIC FROGS AND
A PROPER COPPER COFFEE POT

Phew! No mistakes?

We're almost done. Now you're READY. Oh yes.

You're ready for what experts say is the
TRICKIEST tongue-twister in the whole world...

THE SIXTH SICK SHEIKH'S SIXTH SHEEP'S SICK

Wait - what?!
Looks simple but it's pretty difficult.
Did you manage it?

Anyway, I think your final challenge is MUCH harder than this...

Yes, get ready for the...
MOST TRICKY-TONGUE-TWISTER ever invented!!
And, I should mention, this is absolutely the very FIRST time it has ever appeared in a book!!!

Can you say it all in one go? With no mistakes?
I CAN'T. And I've tried a few times now, believe me...

Anyway, well done for getting this far.
Happy reading.

Happy speaking.

And GOOD LUCK!

You're going to need it...

RED LORRY YELLOW LORRY BLUE BUBB
THE SEASHORE ELEVEN LEMON LOLLIES
THREE THICK THISTLES FORTY-FOUR
FISH SIXTY-SIX SHORT STICKS SEVEN
PUMA BADGER BEAVER OTTER OYSTER
CHIHUAHUA ALPACA ANACONDA BARRACU
GORILLA HYENA KOALA PANTHER PIRA
CLUCK QUACK TWEET BAA BARK CACKL
HONK HOOT HOWL RIBBIT ROAR SCR
TWIT-TWOO BUBBLE BUBBLE DOUBLE B
PUDDLE BABBLE BRAMBLE FIDDLE FUDDLE
POODLE MUMBLE CRUMBLE BOBBLE BUMBL
CHATTER CHOMP CHORTLE CHUCKLE
HICCUP HUM HUSH MOAN MURMUR MUT
SNIFF SNORT SQUEAL WAFFLE WOW W
BANG BASH BEEP BOING BUMP CLANG C
CRACK CRACKLE CRASH CREAK CROAK
GLUG GURGLE PLINK PLONK PLOP PLUCK
RUMBLE RUSTLE SLAP SLIP SLITHER
SPLATTER SPLUTTER SPLISH SPLOSH
THUMP THWACK TINKLE TRICKLE TW
WHIR WHIZ WHOOP WHOOSH ZAP ZIN

LACK BUBBLE SHE SELLS SEASHELLS ON
ENTY-TWO TINY TURTLES THIRTY-
ZEN FRUITCAKES FIFTY-FIVE FIERCE
SEVEN BENEVOLENT ELEPHANTS PANDA
MUR LOBSTER IGUANA IMPALA CICADA
BELUGA CAPYBARA CHINCHILLA GOPHER
QUAGGA QUOKKA TUNA VICUNA BUZZ
W CHEEP CHIRP CUCKOO GOBBLE HISS
SQUAWK WARBLE WHINNY YIP YOWL
E SIZZLE SIZZLE FIZZLE SIZZLE PEBBLE
DLE MUDDLE DOODLE NOODLE STRUDEL
HOO AHEM AHOY AHA BLAB BRRRR BURP
GLE GIGGLE GROAN GRUNT GRUMBLE
SCREAM SHOUT SIGH SLOBBER SLURP
WHISPER YAY YIKES YAWN ZZZZZ BAM
CLASH CLATTER CLICK CLINK CLUNK
UNCH DRIP FIZZ FLICK FLIP FLUTTER
NK POP POW PUFF RATTLE RING RUFF
P SLOSH SMASH SNIP SPLASH SPLAT
UISH SQUELCH SWISH SWOOSH THUD
VROOM WALLOP WHACK WHAM WHIP
P ZOOOOOOOOM BING-BONG DING-

DONG TICK-TOCK CLIP-CLOP CLICKETY
PING-PONG KAPOW KERPLUNK KABOO
BEAR BIG BLACK BUG RUGGED ROCKS P
CAN WOULD A WOODCHUCK CHUCK A
PIPER PICKED A PECK OF PICKLED PEP
BETTER BUTTER BOW BOW BOW BOW
DOG THIN CAT THICK CAT ROLLING R
SLIP SLAP SLOP BLACK BACKED BAT
KNAPSACK STRAPS FORK HANDLES FOU
TOY BOAT TOY BOAT TOY BOAT SHE
SEA A NOISY NOISE ANNOYS AN OYS
NIGHT NURSE NELLY IS NURSING NIC
MOSES SUPPOSES HIS TOESES ARE RO
SOON THIS FRIENDLY PHILIP FLIPS FI
FRYING FRESH FLOUNDER GREEN COW
SHIP-SHIPPING SHIP SHIPPING SHIPPI
PINK AND PURPLE PATCHES WE WENT T
WINKING HORTENSE'S TORTOISE TAUC
BOX OF BISCUITS MIXED BISCUITS BIC
BABY BOTTLE SWISS WRISTWATCH
TURQUOISE TOOTHBRUSH SLIPPERY S
SIXTH SICK SHEIKH'S SIXTH SHEEP'S S

ACK JINGLE-JANGLE PITTER-PATTER
SKUNK SAT ON A STUMP BIG BLACK
EST PUMPKINS WHOSE SHOES CAN A
TOR WHO TOOTED A FLUTE PETER
BETTY BOTTER BOUGHT A BIT OF
ISSUES TENNIS SHOES FIT DOG FAT
AGONS SNAP CRACKLE POP TOP COP
LING GARGOYLES WORLD WIDE WEB
NDLES RED LEATHER YELLOW LEATHER
S CHEESE SEVEN SWANS SWAM IN THE
THE CHEAP SHOP SOLD SHEEP CHOPS
MY MISS MISSY MISSES MISSISSIPPI
SURELY WE SHALL SEE THE SUNSHINE
LAPJACKS THAT FAT FRIAR FRED IS
THER TO GRAZE ON GREEN GRASS A
SHIPS CLEOPATRA'S MATTRESS HAS
ALES TO WATCH WHALES AND WALRUS
US THE IMPORTANCE OF SHORTNESS
TTLE BLUE BOTTLE BROWN BOTTLE
SH WRISTWATCH FRENCH FLIPFLOP
S SILK SKIRTS FRANTIC FROGS THE
AND A PROPER COPPER COFFEE POT

So, there you have it.

EASY WORDS
HARDER WORDS
FUNNY WORDS
CONFUSING WORDS
SHORTISH WORDS AND WOR
LOVELY-LONG-AND-LISTY W

and

TRICKY-TRIP-UP-TANGLED

WORDS

DS LINED NEATLY IN A ROW

-DS THAT

TUMBLE
AS THEY
GO

NOW...
...have yourself a nice lemon lolly
and take the rest of the day off!

THE END
THE END
THE END
THE END

AUTHOR

Huw Lewis-Jones is a writer and teacher who loves words. He has created many books about amazing photographs and explorers with huge beards, but these days his children's stories are mostly about apples and badgers, and a crocodile with a taste for treacle tart. Huw helps his students to overcome their fears of public speaking and for the last decade has even run poetry and limerick competitions in Antarctica. He lives in a little house in Cornwall, with a panda in the garden and seagulls on the roof. His favourite simple twister is ELEVEN LEMON LOLLIES. Delicious!

First published in 2021 by
The British Library
96 Euston Road
London NW1 2DB
www.bl.uk/publishing

ISBN 978 0 7123 5465 3

British Library Cataloguing in Publication Data
A catalogue record for this publication is available from the British Library

Illustrated by Joanna Lisowiec
Designed by Georgie Hewitt
www.igotapapercut-studio.com

Printed and bound by Gutenberg Press, Malta